Lydia Loves to Look at the Stars

Lydia Loves to Look at the Stars
First Edition

Copyright © 2022 by Patricia Cousineau
All rights reserved. Printed in the United States of America.
No part of this book may be used or reproduced in any manner whatsoever without written permission except in the case of brief quotations embodied in critical articles and reviews.

For more information, please contact:
Silk Rhode Books
868 Greenville Ave
Johnston, RI 02919
silkrhodebooks@gmail.com

Library of Congress Control Number: 2022944985
ISBN 978-1-7370446-3-5

Illustrations by Jasper Penn

Lydia Loves to Look at the Stars

Written by Patricia Cousineau
Illustrated by Jasper Penn

I have a friend named Lydia.

She is six years old.

She has blond hair and brown eyes.

She has freckles on her nose
and on her arms.

She has a nice smile.

Lydia lives in Georgia,
a state where it is warm
most of the year.

There are lots of nights when
you can go outside
and look up at the stars.

Lydia's mommy is an artist.

An artist is a person who makes
beautiful things for people to enjoy.

Her mommy makes pictures
with a brush and watercolor paints,
just like the pictures
you are looking at now.

Do you know how Lydia started to love looking at the stars?

Well, I will tell you.

When Lydia was just a little baby, her mommy got to thinking about all the beautiful things she didn't see at night when she was asleep.

So, one night when the sky was very clear and the stars were very bright, her mommy went to Lydia's bedroom and tickled her tummy to wake her up.

Lydia giggled because she loved to have her tummy tickled.

Mommy said she was going
to show Lydia something beautiful
she had never seen before.

She wrapped Lydia up in a warm quilt
and took her out into the back yard.

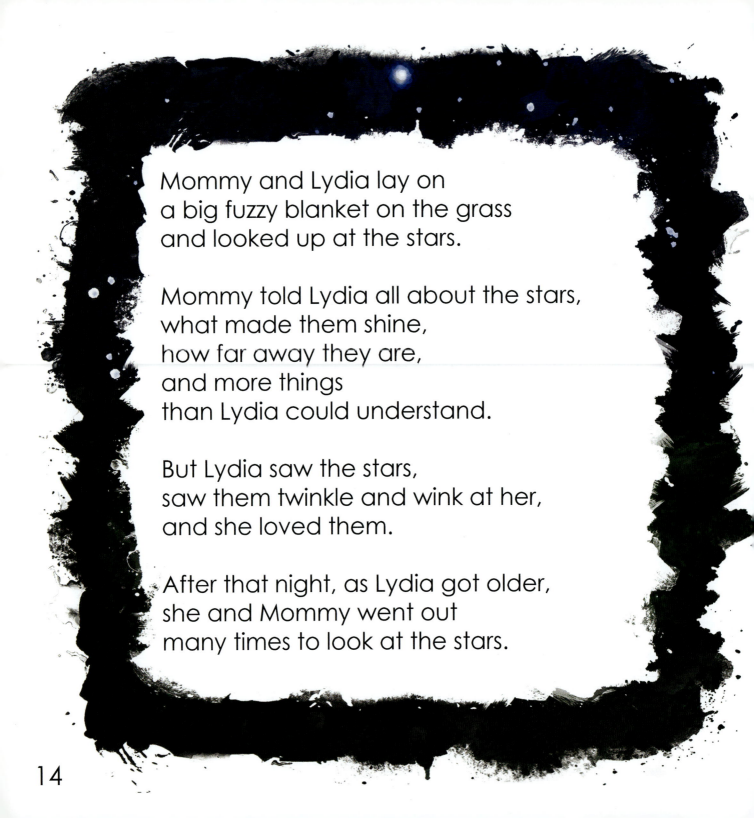

Mommy and Lydia lay on
a big fuzzy blanket on the grass
and looked up at the stars.

Mommy told Lydia all about the stars,
what made them shine,
how far away they are,
and more things
than Lydia could understand.

But Lydia saw the stars,
saw them twinkle and wink at her,
and she loved them.

After that night, as Lydia got older,
she and Mommy went out
many times to look at the stars.

After that night,
Lydia and her mommy went out
many times to look at the stars.

Sometimes she thinks
they look like diamond necklaces
hanging across the sky.

Sometimes she thinks
they look like flashlights
in the hands of hundreds of angels.

Sometimes she thinks
they look like her mommy's
black and white polka-dot scarf.

Lydia's teacher said some people make pictures from the stars like connect-the-dots puzzles.

Lydia likes to look at the stars
in different ways.

Sometimes she lies on her back
in the grass.

Sometimes she uses her telescope and looks from her bedroom window.

Sometimes she sits on the porch swing and looks up.

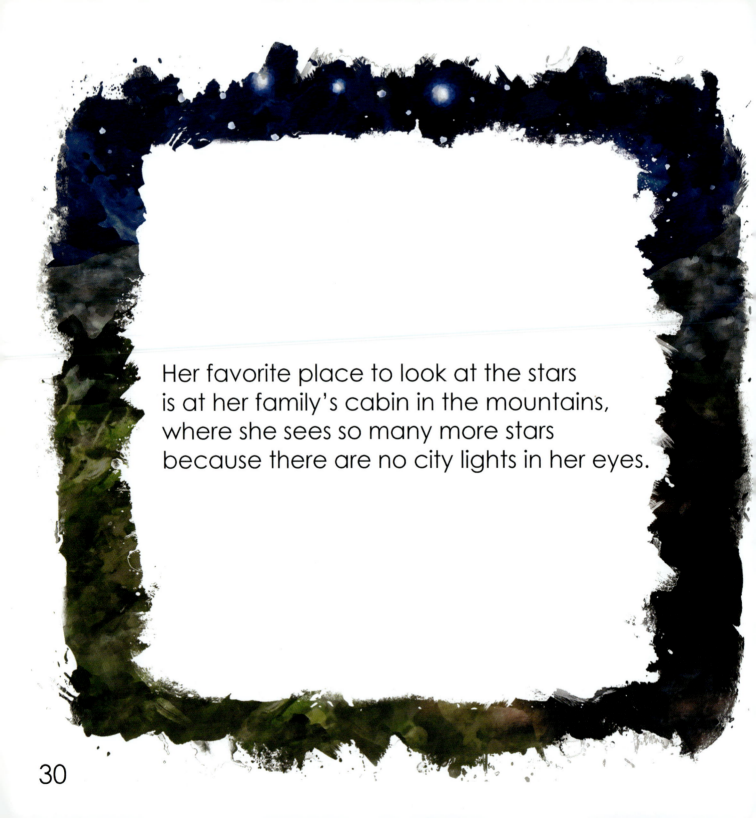

Her favorite place to look at the stars
is at her family's cabin in the mountains,
where she sees so many more stars
because there are no city lights in her eyes.

I think if you pass by Lydia's backyard
on a very clear, very starry night,
you just might see Lydia
and her mommy out there
on a fuzzy blanket
looking up at the sky
and enjoying the stars.

What do you see when
you look at the stars?

The End